The Woolgatherers

ALSO BY ARTHUR H. VEASEY III

Sweet Lorraine

A Reasonable Doubt

The Diary of Dolly Makepeace

The Woolgatherers

ARTHUR H. VEASEY III

THE WOOLGATHERERS
Copyright © 2024 by Arthur H. Veasey III. All rights reserved.

This book is a work of fiction. Names, characters, places and incidents are either products of the author's imagination or used fictitiously. Any resemblance to actual events, locales, or persons, living or dead, is entirely coincidental. No part of this publication can be reproduced or transmitted in any form or by any means, electronic or mechanical, without permission in writing from the author or publisher.

For Virginia and Larssen

CHAPTER 1

The Dreamer

The smell of the harbor was the first thing she remembered. It was not an unpleasant smell, but rather an ageless odor that declared Boothbay was a fisherman's town and not just some yachtsman's port of call. Its people were decent, hardworking folks, who greeted the summer residents genially, but breathed a sigh of relief when they went home after Labor Day. Pier 8 was busy with tourists and Islanders competing on the narrow gangway for the one hour excursion aboard the *Kickshaw*, a forty-seven foot vessel that also served as primary transportation to and from Bushytail Isle. Emma boarded routinely and soon the familiar sights of McFarland, Tumbler, and Burnt Island Light lifted her spirits into a new season, on the very day when the end of spring intersected perfectly with the beginning of summer.

A mackerel sky stretched as far as the eye could see, a sure sign of a change in the weather her grandfather always said. Pot buoys bobbed impatiently as each passing wave heaved a heavy sigh before the sea took it back. The ocean was formless, unfathomable, and chaotic she thought as she stared out at the horizon, yet it also embodied stability as it had existed largely unchanged for centuries. So too, her destination. Bushytail was somehow locked in time, not in an antiquated or obsolete way—more like a cocoon in which life slows down, less is more, and small moments are precious.

Compared to other summer colonies Bushytail was tiny—just over a hundred cottages with no cars or bikes, and there weren't any stores or movie theaters. Instead, there was a pallid rocky shoreline with two small sandy beaches, and a cove crowded with boats, and a float where dock diving was a favorite sport. There were organized activities from tennis to kayaking but for the most part, Island kids made their own fun. *No rocks no docks,* was the rule that her parents posted when she was a little girl, but other than that Emma could hang out with friends and roam the Island all day and into dusk so long as she made it home by curfew.

As they neared the landing, Emma recognized her grandfather standing on the wharf above the ferry dock. She yelled and waved her arms frantically until he spied her and let out a whistle. A few of her friends stayed hidden then surprised her at the freight shed. On Bushytail you took no risk stepping forward and giving a kiss, so she greeted each with outstretched arms.

The truck guys moved in quickly, loading her belongings onto a Chevy pickup that had seen better days before her grandfather waved her onward. "C'mon Emma, you can hang out with your friends soon enough, you have a lot of unpacking ahead of you."

Emma gave her friends another hug. "I'll meet up with you guys tomorrow, we have a lot of catching up to do."

The Steele family cottage was near the middle of the Island but had distant views toward Linekin Bay to the east and Southport to the west. A classic Maine cottage with four bedrooms and a porch that wrapped around three sides, it had never been painted but time had turned cedar shingles a deep rich brown that suited it among the surrounding pine stands. Emma's bedroom was standard with exposed studs painted a mid-century pink turned salmon with age. After supper, she unpacked the last of her bags and then collapsed onto the familiar mattress before closing her eyes. The train ride from New York to Boston to Portland had tired her, and now that the excitement of seeing her friends had worn away, the onrushing sleep came swiftly, like a late afternoon squall.

Emma's mind drifted, clouded with vague images until she became gradually aware of a chamber, softly illuminated by row after row of small votive candles like the ones her mother taught her to light at church. The room was filled with oddities—shiny goblets, flags she had never seen before, even an hourglass. Beyond were several vertical windows through which one could see the stars. As her eyes adjusted to the darkness, a figure emerged, only faintly visible through slender shafts of moonlight. A kerchief stretched across his forehead, and he wore a waistcoat with wide knee-length trousers. He glanced her way, then balked when a seagull, coasting on a bed of wind, gave out a plaintive cry.

Emma awakened with a jolt, her muscles gradually coming to life as she pulled the blanket around her neck. Through squares of blue darkness of open windows, came the distant sound of waves beating on the shore. Her eyes fixed on dimly lit numerals across the room—4:30 AM. She had slept fitfully, but her mind was racing, and she could not fall back asleep. This ghost or whatever it was, was more intriguing than alarming she thought, and she wanted to find out what it all meant. Time to get up she decided, sunrise was just half an hour away and her grandfather was an early riser. She liked conversing with him because he knew a lot of Island history—plus he usually rustled up a pretty good breakfast of scrambled eggs and bacon.

·   ·   ·

Grandfather listened patiently as Emma described as many of the details that she could recall from the dream. He knew that she had an intellectually curious side to her that he encouraged. She liked to dig a little more deeply than most into a situation and consider the facts before making judgments or drawing conclusions. In this case her story seemed more than a fantasy and her observations struck him as sincere enough to deserve his attention.

"Do you have any idea what this spirit portrayed—a real person or something more mystical?"

"I have no idea, a person I guess. Then there was this annoying squawk from a passing seagull."

Grandfather tarried over his eggs for a moment—something he did every so often before offering a thought.

"Your description of your dream actually makes me think of a pirate's den."

"I thought the same thing Grandfather, but I didn't want it to sound like I was channeling Jack Sparrow or something."

"Well, have you been reading any books or watching something on the History Channel that might have caused you to subconsciously fixate on pirates?"

"No" she shook her head, I thought about that, and I can't think of a single thing that might cause this phantom to invade my psyche."

Grandfather paused and poured more coffee into his mug then rubbed his thumb and forefingers across his chin.

"So, these dreams began when you were convalescing from that awful ski accident you had last February, then intensified as winter turned to spring, correct?" Emma nodded. "And now just as you arrive at the Island you have the most vivid one of all—not a nightmare mind you, but something intense and pretty personal."

"Yes, and this time I think it tried to communicate with me."

"So maybe it *was* a pirate and his parrot," he winked.

"We're not in Port Royal, Grandfather, and it wasn't a parrot, it was a noisy, red-eyed seagull," she said dryly.

"Pirates weren't only plotting their mischief in the Caribbean, Emmy. Why there are stories of them up and down the Maine coast and at least one of them made a raid on Pemaquid. I think his name was Dixie Bull."

"Really? I never heard about this. Where can I learn more about this Dixie Bull? This is so interesting Grandfather, I want to know more."

"Start at our Library, they have a good collection of books about the history of the Maine coast. It's also possible that the Maritime Museum in Bath has something, and they operate a small reference library. Best to contact them ahead of time to let them know what you're researching. And remember—the written materials that you uncover will be a great resource, but don't dismiss oral testimony especially when it comes to local history."

Emma wasted little time in conducting her research mostly at the library but also with some online links that the Maritime Museum provided. She learned that Dixie Bull started out as an honest trader dealing in mostly beaver fur and blankets along the Maine coast. After his shallop was attacked in Penobscot Bay by a band of French corsairs who stole all his goods and provisions, the incident so angered him that he turned to piracy to recoup his losses. His reputation was sealed one day when he sailed into Pemaquid Harbor with three sloops, opened fire on the stockade, and sacked the town. What became of him after that is a matter for speculation. Some stories claimed he joined up with the French, while others said that he sailed to England, where he was hanged for piracy. Emma was not convinced that she had uncovered everything she needed to know, so she started browsing random websites when a cryptic footnote appeared on an abandoned online chatroom about pirates in North America. "Have chart—treasure hidden in a cavern on an island—possibly Damariscove or Island of second sight."

The comment was old and unsupported by sources, yet Emma felt as though she had uncovered an important clue. If this were true it placed her pirate right in her own backyard. Why you could see several of those islands from the south shore, and she had sailed by Damariscove many times. She looked for a name or a handle to the missive. "*Red Dog 49.*"

CHAPTER 2

Red Dog 49

Emma had to confide in someone, there were too many pieces to this puzzle for one girl to solve by herself. Dennis Clark was the right person she was sure, quiet but smart, and he knew how to keep a secret. His home was in Portland, so he knew the area well. More importantly, he had a boat that they could use to do a little gunkholing. It was an old 16' Boston Whaler with a reliable engine that could get them safely to the outer Harbor Islands and back.

"So that's my mystery, Dennis. I can't help but think there might be some risk in this investigation so if you don't want to get involved, I'll understand."

"Are you kidding? I've always dreamed about being a treasure hunter and if there's a little danger along the way, I'm your man. So, when do we start?"

"Tomorrow. I want you to take me to the Maritime Museum. There's an archivist there who I think can help us. She has access to a lot of the details concerning Dixie Bull's raid on Pemaquid and she also claims to have connections to a few of the old salts that are known to possess oral histories."

The ride to Bath was both scenic and exhilarating from the back of Dennis' motorcycle. The machine had foot pedals that allowed Emma to stabilize her weight and she adjusted quickly, leaning into the turns. The hum of the engine was like a song to her ears and the ride passed quickly before they arrived at their destination.

Inside, the museum buzzed with visitors and sightseers queued up for the next tour. After paying for admission, they cut the line and deftly navigated their way to the Research and Education Center. An attractive middle-aged woman wearing half readers glanced up as they approached.

"Can I help you?"

"Yes, my name is Emma Steele, I have an appointment to see one of the museum archivists."

"Oh yes Emma, I'm Robin Grant—I've been expecting you."

"It's nice to meet you Robin, this is my friend Dennis, and we are so grateful for your time."

"So, you mentioned that you are interested in the Dixie Bull attack on Pemaquid, and I am sure you've read the historical accounts, what more can I do to assist you?"

"I read somewhere that he may have visited Damariscove Island. I'm curious to learn more about that rumor and whether his exploration might have been documented. I'm especially anxious to learn if he might have set foot on any of the other islands near Boothbay."

"Meaning Bushytail Isle," Robin remarked absently.

"Well yes, I have a hunch that he may have made other landfalls within the region possibly on Bushytail. It was uninhabited at the time and could have served as a safe harbor from privateers giving chase after one of his raids."

Robin's eyes instinctively searched the computer screen for any links.

"The journey to Damariscove Island was recorded in the diary of one Gavin Ogg, a Scotsman who reportedly sailed with Dixie Bull when his ship was attacked by the French in Penobscot Bay. His entries mention other islands sighted on the return voyage, but it would be difficult to identify Bushytail since it was not yet so named. Seaman Ogg was among those who returned to Boston Harbor but there is no mention on the manifest that he remained with the crew when it departed, which makes me think that he may have been conscripted into piracy."

"May I see the diary?"

"I'm afraid we lost track of it. It was never the museum's property in the first place, it belonged to a descendent who moved away from the area—let me look up his name."

It was a few clicks of the keyboard before she found what she was looking for: "Richard D. Ogg, retired Naval Intelligence Officer, later a college professor at Berkley after moving to California. He'd be a hundred years old now if he were still alive."

"Does it say if he had any children?" Robin paused for several minutes before retrieving the record.

"R. Davidson Ogg, Jr., last known residence Kodiak, Alaska."

.   .   .

"Kodiak, Alaska—holy cow!" Dennis exclaimed as he grabbed his helmet for the ride back to Boothbay. "I somehow thought your old salt would at least be in the same time zone."

"That certainly makes things more complicated. Let's think—how do we go about locating and reaching out to someone three thousand miles away?"

"Who may or may not have any information that's of value to us and may not even be alive."

"Oh, I think he's alive all right, and if our friend Robin Grant is right about all this, we may have hit the jackpot." Dennis gave her a puzzled look.

"How so?"

Emma pulled on her helmet and clipped the chinstrap before answering: "The alias of our chatroom user was '*Red Dog 49*,' correct? Well, when people think up a handle like that, they often use key words that are codes for their actual identity. I knew we'd found our man as soon as Robin identified the surviving descendent as Mr. R. D. Ogg from our 49th state, Alaska." Dennis' jaw dropped.

"Emma, you really are a super sleuth."

.   .   .

Grandfather was attentive as Emma recounted her visit to the museum and what she had deduced from her investigations. "Whoever has the diary must also possess the map, at least that is what I infer from *Red Dog 49*'s post. I feel like we are so close, but I have yet to figure out how to locate this Mr. Ogg, a continent away. I will do a Google search and if by chance he's still in Kodiak I might find an address or phone number to track him down. Even if I'm successful I'm not sure how I'll introduce myself or explain to him the crazy reason for my intrusion."

"I know Davidson Ogg," Grandfather announced matter-of-factly "he was my classmate at Newfield Academy." Emma was dumbfounded.

"You what? Are you sure we're talking about the same person? I mean this guy lives in Alaska."

"I'm quite certain it's him. Dave was a free spirit—he moved there right after college and became a salmon fisherman. He still fishes commercially but he has several other successful business enterprises around Kodiak Island."

"Do you keep in touch with him?"

"He occasionally contributes to our class notes in the alumni magazine, but I haven't had any direct contact with him for years. Let me reach out to our class secretary, he more than likely has an email address for him, and I can help you with an introduction."

By nightfall, Emma's mind was spinning again. In a matter of days, she had uncovered a lead that could prove not only Dixie Bull's presence at Damariscove but could conceivably reveal clues to the location of a hidden treasure. Her head hit the pillow and her dreams propelled her to a sandy shore with a wooden hulk, half buried. She wanted to free the vessel from its grave, but a relentless tide brought an unending flow of sand around her feet. With each futile shovel full taken, ten yards more of beach returned. She became anxious and confounded as a flock of gulls swarmed chaotically about her head, their cries a cacophony of protest, amidst a plaintive bleating from the grassy meadow above.

· · ·

It was Sunday and Emma spied Dennis outside the Chapel and waved him over for a chat and to inform him of the latest turn of events.

"My grandfather sent an email to his classmate Mr. Ogg, explaining our circumstances, which I hope will lead us into a conversation. I'd love to know more about the contents of the diary, and I particularly want to learn more about the map. In the meantime, I am eager to pay Erika a visit to see what the Island Historical Society might be able to provide that will add to add to our list of clues."

"What can she tell us? I thought all the evidence was pointing us toward Damariscove."

"Maybe yes, maybe no. Red Dog's missive said that pirates buried treasure somewhere in a cave. The only caves I've ever heard of around this neck of the woods are located right here at Cutter Point."

Erika was a summer intern from South Carolina in her third year of residence on the Island. She was seated outside the Post Office when the two Island gumshoes arrived seeking her assistance, peppering her with questions and prodding her knowledge of the caves.

"Well, there is some debate about those caves among Island historians. Some claim the Navy used them during World War II as U-boat range-finding bunkers. Others say they were glacier caves prone to collapse and that they were intentionally demolished to prevent any accidents."

"Has anyone been up there to have a look for themselves?" Dennis asked.

"Not to my knowledge. Angus Williams told me he scaled those cliffs as a boy and found the caves to be barely accessible. But he passed away two years ago, and I can't think of anyone else who might have been so daring." Emma thanked Erika for her help, before heading to the boathouse.

"Keep me informed of your progress, I'm so interested," Erika called out.

Dennis raced ahead to the cove and was already easing the whaler into the float by the time she arrived.

"The forecast calls for rainy weather tomorrow so let's head over to Cutter Point while it's still daylight," Emma said. "I'd like to see if we can get a clear view of the cave entrance from the water. I also need to take some photos to figure out how one of us can get up there to find out if there is access to whatever cavern lies within that cliff."

The tide flooded the shoreline as they rounded the eastern point of the Island, so Dennis was careful of the rising swells, slowly navigating to less turbulent waters. The cliffs rose vertically, sporadically covered with lichen and moss, a stark contrast to the bleached granite rocks that hemmed much of the Island's shoreline. There appeared to be a dark sheltered area about 30 feet or so above the high-water mark, and Emma raised her binoculars for a closer inspection.

"That must be it—I can see an entrance that looks to be about three or four feet wide in breadth but not very high. There's a lot of blunted, knobby stones around or near the opening and there is a definite ingress, but I can't tell if there is a passage." Emma reached for her camera and attached a telephoto lens before shooting multiple frames of the yawning mouth on the face of the cliff.

"We're rapidly losing our light, let's head back and we can download these pictures to my computer."

As they prepared to depart, the purr of the engine was interrupted from above by a rapid sound of squeaks and clicks. An instant later a flight of seabirds emerged from the cliff, zigzagging through the twilight, incited by the discordant cry of a solitary seagull.

"Well, someone calls our cave home," Dennis quipped. "I hope you're not afraid of birds."

"I think that's called ornithophobia. I know they are usually harmless, but I generally avoid them."

CHAPTER 3

A Pirate's Journal

On Monday a light rain fell, and fog surrounded the Island. Most of Emma's friends escaped to the Harbor for pizza and a movie. Emma and Dennis remained behind since her grandfather had arranged a phone call for them to speak with his old boarding school chum. Four hours separated Alaskan Time Zone from Eastern Daylight Time so Dave Ogg's coffee break in Kodiak coincided with lunchtime at Bushytail. The phone rang and Emma answered just as the siren sounded from the farmhouse.

"Davidson Ogg here."

"Hello Mr. Ogg, this is Emma Steele speaking from Bushytail Isle, Maine and I have my friend Dennis Clark with me."

"Greetings from Kodiak, Alaska Emma and Dennis. It is my pleasure to speak with the granddaughter of a friend from so many years removed. Your grandfather's email filled me in on the reason for this conversation—what more can I tell you about my ancestor Gavin Ogg?"

"Thank you, we don't want to waste your time so let me start with a few questions that we think are central to our investigation. First, in what way do you believe your ancestor's diary proves unequivocally that he sailed with Dixie Bull during his reign of piracy in Pemaquid and this region?"

"Well, unequivocally is too finite a word when one is interpreting journal entries written three hundred years ago, young lady. However, the content of his entries are organized as a collection that range over the precise period that Dixie Bull was accused of piracy, and each entry holds content that support the thoughts and recollections of a sailor whose voyages at sea were active in the acts of piracy."

"The diary implies that they made for Damariscove Island sometime after the Pemaquid raid. The booty seized from the raid was reported to have been £55. That hardly seems like a treasure."

"What the records do not show is that shortly after the attack on Pemaquid, Dixie Bull captured, then burned a Spanish Galleon bound for Cádiz that was laden with gold, silver, and other goods. When news of the piracy reached Boston, they mistakenly thought that the more notorious William Kidd was to blame, and orders were sent out to pursue and arrest him and his accomplices for piracy.

Meanwhile, Dixie and his crew set sail for a group of Islands he had spied near Boothbay where deep water and safe harbors kept them hidden from their enemies. Gavin Ogg's entry is the only surviving testimony of the affair which was later authenticated in documents pertaining to Captain Kidd's trial in London."

"And what of the property stolen from the Spanish Galleon?"

"Dixie took most of his plunder with him when he left the region for New Foundland, never to be heard from again. It was around this time my ancestor Gavin Ogg, having forsaken piracy, deserted ship during a port of call at Machias. Bull's crew caught up with him, beat him brutally, and left him for dead. But not until he disclosed in his journal that he had hidden a cache of treasure inside a cavern on an island, somewhere along the Maine coast, and I believe he survived the assault to reclaim it. If you can locate the…. cartographer… by the…"

Without warning a weak signal began causing their conversation to break up, cutting out intermittently, followed by three short beeps before the connection was dropped. Emma tried calling back without success.

"I guess my remaining questions will have to wait for another day," Emma said dolefully. "At least we know that this crazy pirate's tale has some basis of fact behind it. Now if we can just learn more about the map."

"I'm afraid that will have to wait," Grandfather interrupted "Dave told me in his email that he leaves for an extended salmon fishing trip tomorrow. He will be incommunicado for at least a month."

. . .

A hive of activity fronted the Post Office when Emma arrived to seek out Erika. She intended to browse through the records for more information about the caves when a voice called out.

"Emma, Emma Steele, there's a mail tube, that just arrived, marked "Priority." It's addressed to you, all the way from Alaska," shouted the postmaster. "Cost the sender $15.95 to get it here so it must be pretty important." Emma rushed inside and quickly accepted delivery before hastening for home. Dennis intercepted her along the route where she held out the cardboard cylinder for inspection.

"What do you think is in there?"

"I don't know but let's not waste any time finding out."

Inside the cottage, Dennis used a small pocketknife to open one end of the tube, reached inside with two fingers, and dexterously removed the contents. It was some sort of document that appeared to be old but not fragile. Bound with a red ribbon it contained a handwritten note slipped in between. Dennis handed the dispatch to Emma, and she read it aloud.

Emma: Sorry our discussion was cut short. I am enclosing this chart, which has been handed down, through many generations of my family. I have no direct descendants, so I now entrust this to you. Your grandfather has described your curious intellect in such a way that I am confident that you are the most deserving person to follow this ancestral journey to its conclusion. Good luck and my sincere best wishes, ~D.O.

Hardly a word was spoken as they unrolled the map and carefully spread it out across the kitchen table. The paper seemed sturdy and rather cotton-like with distinct patterns of vertical lines. There were traces of binding as though it had been carefully removed from a ship's log or journal. The map was crudely defined without any color except for a brownish tint that spread unevenly across the surface. *Booth Bay, Damariscotta,* and *Newagen* were clearly labeled along with *Monheigin Island east of Pemaquid*.

"It's the old English spelling" Emma whispered as she held a magnifying glass carefully above the ancient map, "I can make out Southport and a few small unidentified land masses, but there's nothing remarkable here as far as I can tell, except—wait a minute." At the bottom of the map scrawled in tiny longhand text, Emma's eye caught something that appeared to be a navigational notation:

At midnight got a distance from two stars–gave the Lat. abt. 43.81 N & Long. 69.63 W

"Dennis, what are the coordinates for Bushytail?"

"43.8081 North and 69.6301 West, why do you ask?"

"Because, if this is a treasure map then we are ground zero."

CHAPTER 4

The Cipher

A week raced by, and Emma was restless and wanted to restart their cave exploration. The entrance had to be examined firsthand to decide if it could be safely accessed before any spelunking could be attempted. Dennis was experienced in rock climbing from an Outward Bound program he had taken, and he had sufficient gear to scale the face of the cliff. After planning their assault, the pair made their way down a narrow trail that led to the small inlet at Cutter Point where they traversed the rocky shoreline. Dennis took his time planning his ascent as he had been taught. Using the features and irregularities in the granite rock, he edged his way up the nearly vertical face of the cliff seeking out the crags and vegetation that would aid his climb toward the cave entrance. He was steadily advancing and less than ten feet away from his objective when a dive-bombing seagull strafed him from above. Instinctively he ducked, losing his balance for an instant, before reaching for a crack in the cliff face where he held on long enough to maneuver his body to a better position. Emma gasped in fright before guessing at the cause of the bird's aggression.

"Dennis, move carefully but deliberately away from the shrubbery," she shouted, "there may be chicks nesting in there." Dennis did as he was told moving laterally to a point where he no longer posed a threat to any feathered squatters. He took several breaths to slow down his heart rate while staring out at the ocean for a minute or so before resuming his climb. Finding an alternative course, he nimbly circumnavigated his way to the cave entrance and hoisted himself to a shelf at the opening. Turning on the headlamp that stretched across his forehead, he peered into the expanse for a few minutes before calling down to Emma. "I'm going in." A moment later he disappeared from view to Emma's mixed emotions of excitement and trepidation. Inside, he crawled on his stomach through a narrow portal for a short distance before the walls expanded into an open cavern. He estimated the room was about 30 feet wide with a somewhat greater depth and was dank and musty. He allowed his headlamp to move slowly across the cavity for any sign of human disturbance but saw nothing. For several more minutes, he searched with his eyes for other passages or enclaves, but the grotto revealed no secrets. He glanced upward—a colony of bats hung from the ceiling, unmoved by his intrusion. *Sleeping at midday* he thought to himself, *it's probably a good idea to leave this sanctum sooner than later.* Dennis squinted toward the afterglow that signaled the way out when his quarrelsome seagull abruptly screamed through the entry. Dennis wheeled to avoid the bird's flight and lost his balance, stumbling to the floor of the cave. Straightening his headlamp, he brushed himself off and regained a hunched stance. About six feet away the gull rested on one leg, observing him with muted interest. Grey wings highlighted a bright white breast. It lithely narrowed its tail feathers then stretched its throat and beak forward, before extending a second thin yellow leg to the ground, sweeping away the mossy floor with its triangular webbed foot. It repeated this behavior for about thirty seconds before returning its beady stare toward Dennis. *He almost seems to be telling me something,* he thought. *How shall I respond?* Dennis slowly lowered his body to a squatting position and held out his hand. The bird tilted his head slightly displaying a peculiar red iris that surrounded a dark pupil, before setting off with jackknifed wings toward daylight, the same way it had arrived.

Dennis took in a deep breath then slowly expelled the damp air—something important had just happened but he didn't know what. The clues were somewhere in the cave he just had to figure them out. He looked down to where the gull had performed its dance ritual. Years of previously undisturbed moss and lichen were scraped away revealing some kind of markings, like the hieroglyphics of ancient Egyptians but with more modern symbols. He rubbed away more cave moss to reveal what appeared to be a combination of blocks and letters scratched into the bedrock like a mathematical equation. *This is some kind of cipher* he thought to himself as he examined the markings. He spent about ten minutes committing to memory each of the symbols before him, then made his way back outside and into the late afternoon sun. The air was refreshing but windy, so he wrapped a climbing rope around a rock allowing both ends to touch the ground so that he could retrieve it, after lowering himself to the flat earth below.

"You were in there for a long time, I was quite worried" Emma scolded, "What did you see—did you uncover any clues? Tell me at once, I am so curious." Dennis answered with a wide grin.

·　　·　　·

Grandfather listened attentively as the two Island sleuths divulged their findings, seeking his advice. Dennis sketched from memory the encryption he had uncovered in the cave. They were stumped by the cipher with its confusing symbols, grids, and elements. Emma knew her grandfather was a Freemason and she remembered him telling her that their oath of secrecy was guarded by ciphers meant to keep their rituals concealed.

"The Masonic Cipher is a geometric cipher, which exchanges letters for symbols to create encrypted messages. It consists of a 26-character key, which replaces every character in the alphabet with a different symbol. But the cipher that you have uncovered is more complex to my eye. Without the key, it will be almost impossible to decode."

"So, the cipher key is the information needed to solve the cipher—numbers, letters, and symbols that we can substitute for readable information," Dennis concluded.

"It sounds like it is more important to find the key than the cipher itself," Emma mused, "and without it, we're back to square one."

"Well, it's a roadblock but you've made progress. At least you know that you are on the right trail and not at a dead end."

"So how should we go about uncovering this key?" Dennis asked.

"I have no suggestions," Grandfather replied, "but you two seem to be pretty good at problem solving, so if you will excuse me, I have chores to do."

. . .

Emma and Dennis browsed the Internet for an hour learning as much as they could about the history of ciphers before heading to the hotel beach. It was a warm, sunny day and they needed a break from this puzzle, if only to clear their minds of the myriad of detailed clues that had consumed their thoughts for the past week. Several friends whom they had ignored during their investigation stopped to say hello and renew Island bonds.

"Where have you two been keeping yourselves?" Judy Thompson demanded. "We've missed you guys, and our Thursday night trivia games aren't the same without you." Emma found Judy to be friendly enough, but a bit of a nosey *you-know-what*.

"We've been busy doing a little Island research, something my grandfather asked us to pursue," she fibbed.

"Well, you missed out on a fascinating day—we went to the Harbor last week in the rain, skipped the movie, and drove down to the Bath Iron Works to see a Zumwalt class destroyer that was launched there. It looked so strange, like a big floating trapezoid. It's the first fully electric-powered ship in the Navy and it has stealth-like features and super modern equipment, that includes a newly developed naval intelligence and communication system."

"We will make it up on another occasion, Judy—next rainy day, I promise." Emma chatted with a few other beach-goers before catching Dennis' eye and signaling that it was time to depart.

"Why did we have to leave so soon? I was just starting to work on my tan.

"Your tan is my sunburn—besides I had an epiphany."

"A what?"

"Epiphany—It's Greek for 'Aha!' I had an 'Aha' moment." Dennis knew Emma enough to let her go on without interruption. "As soon as Judy uttered the words *naval intelligence* it struck me all at once. When Robin Grant told us that Mr. Ogg's father was the first person to share the diary with the museum, she explicitly mentioned that he was a Naval Intelligence Officer during World War II."

"So?"

"So, he was a very smart man who collected and analyzed vital information for the Navy, and later became a research instructor at the University of California at Berkley—someone who would have been inclined to study our cipher and solve the key to its translation."

"And if he's like any college professor I've ever known he would have recorded it someplace, like a footnote or some other annotation."

"Exactly," agreed Emma.

CHAPTER 5

The Salmon Drifter

Dave Ogg was an original. The kind of fellow you met once in your life and never forgot. He hailed from Treasure Island, Maine, the perfect allegory for a free spirit who would plot his own life's course. At Newfield, he was an enigmatic and dilatory student, but a surprisingly good athlete who left an indelible impression on his classmates. He furthered his education for two years at Menlo College on the West Coast before wanderlust drove him north toward America's last great frontier. He found his first job one half hour after getting off the ferry in Kodiak at a cannery, butchering King Crab. The cannery work was long hours, starting at six a.m. and going till midnight. Butchering crabs was simple enough; it had a six to ten-inch shell with legs two feet and greater. Grab them out of the stack, put their teeth on the face of an inverted axe, and pull with both hands, separating the claws and legs from the body. Most of the workers were young, college, and high school age, and some were fishermen's wives. Dave found the inhabitants to his liking and decided to make Kodiak his home. By the time Emma's grandfather had reunited with him he was a lawyer, adjunct professor at the University of Alaska, and two-term mayor of the largest city on Kodiak Island. But he reclaimed his inner self every summer, harvesting wild salmon in Bristol Bay aboard his fifty-foot vessel *Sitka*.

"I'm losing patience with this damned bird," he said to Hanta, his longtime friend and first mate. "These buggers follow the offshore fishing boats all the time but this one is relentless. He lagged us for the better part of four days, and I found him on the top of the wheelhouse this morning. Strangest thing—he looked directly at me with that one red eye. I've seen him once before I think, after my father died when we scattered his ashes to the sea off Monterey."

"Inua," Hanta responded. "My people say that your creature carries a spirit that exists in all people, animals, mountains, lakes, and so forth. Not one individual soul, but a chain that connects the communal life and spirit of all that is, has been, and is yet to be."

"Well, whatever he is he's causing me worry, and I can't say exactly why. I dreamt last night about my young friends in Maine who are doing a little research into my forgotten forebear. They were calling out to me from a dory, but I couldn't reach them. Every time I got close this red-eyed mollymawk flew between, and they vanished into the waves. I'm concerned about them, Hanta."

"We are 200 miles from home Captain Dave and incapable of communicating with anyone beyond the fishing fleet—the subconscious mind and the spirit within may be channeling your visions."

"To my point Hanta—*they* cannot communicate directly with *me*. If Inua is personified by this gull, then perhaps his spirit is a messenger. Tell me Hanta, according to your oral tradition could a dead person be reincarnated into a bird?"

"The Inuit believe that all things have a spirit or soul just like humans. These spirits are held to persist even after death. Since all beings possess souls, killing an animal is little different from killing a person and vice versa. Once the spirit of the dead is liberated, it is free to take any form."

"That's a fascinating notion. Do you think acts of passion from these souls could be perpetuated three hundred years later?" Hanta shrugged his shoulders.

"I only know the path of the spirit is never ending."

. . .

Someone once said *a ship in harbor is safe, but that is not what a ship is built for*. In the late-evening twilight of the Alaskan summer, Hanta spotted a jumping sockeye from the bow of the boat and Dave and his crew quickly unfurled

1,200 feet of net from the stern deck in the choppy waters off the mouth of the Naknek River. Gusty winds had prompted most of the fishing boats to set their anchors, while the intrepid *Sitka* drifted aimlessly before encountering a "wall of fish" and 1,500 sockeye salmon hit their net. It was the largest single salmon haul in Dave's lifetime. By midnight he was fatigued but elated when he spied the red-eyed avian perched nearby on the seine boom.

"There you are again my friend," he said under his breath, "if you are a spirit, today you were a good spirit. But your fickle nature troubles me—what is it that compels you to follow me in my sleep and stir up that, which disturbs my friends' work down east?" The gull cocked its head like a dog staring at its owner, then hopped over the boom as if too lazy to spread its white-grey wings. Alighting the cargo hatch, it pranced and danced long yellow legs across a coat of fishy slime that persisted from the evening catch until, after a spell, it raised its body lightly into the night air to a hovering position before taking flight. *I've never seen anything like that before* he thought to himself, *a bird that moon walks.* Dave rested a minute more before nudging his weary legs toward the cabin where his berth beckoned. Glancing downward he paused for a moment to inspect the pattern of figures haphazardly scratched across the hatch cover. *What the heck?* He leaned over for a closer inspection. A sketch of familiar but time-lapsed symbols stared back at him—codes that his father had shown him when he was a boy. *Well, I'll be darned.* Dave's memory flashed back to an occurrence many decades earlier. Men with mysterious accents had come to their home demanding that his father disclose some top-secret information. He always assumed it was military related but never knew for sure. All he remembered was that after the interrogators departed his father had carefully transcribed cryptic information onto an old family seafarer's chart. He showed it to his son, pressed his index finger to his lips, and gave a wink before carefully storing the document back inside a long green lockbox.

.   .   .

Port Moller was remote, but it was the nearest fish processing plant where they could offload their catch, get a fair market price, and head for home. It was also a place to shower and find a warm meal at the small local Inn. Cell phone coverage was spotty, but it existed, so Dave used the opportunity to try to place a call to Emma.

"Hello Emma, it's Davidson Ogg calling from Alaska, can you hear me?"

"Why yes, I can hear you, Mr. Ogg. The signal is not strong but good enough."

"I will make this quick as I am fearful of losing this connection. Have you and your chum discovered any hidden messages during your investigation? More specifically a cipher for which the underlying riddle cannot be cracked."

"Yes, oh yes there was a seagull in the cave at Cutter Point that led Dennis to its discovery—but how did you know?"

"Ah yes, the gull—that reveals a great deal, but I will explain that later. In the meantime, I assume you have the chart that I mailed to you."

"Yes, it arrived earlier this month."

"Very good. In the lower right-hand corner, I have reason to believe my father wrote down the solution to the encryption using a German devised invisible ink. If you very carefully heat the paper the characters should become legible."

"This is the break we've been waiting for—thank you so much."

"Everything happens for a reason Emma. You and Dennis must be vigilant as you continue this journey as there may be conflicting forces in play that could jeopardize the outcome. The gull you encountered is a symbol of intuition. It sees fish before the sailors see them and is a bird of swift movement and decisive action. Should you encounter this bird again, treat it as a spiritual sign. Should it lead you back to its nesting site explore it but be watchful for unseen rivals."

"I'm not sure I understand you Mr. Ogg. What do you mean by conflicting forces? And the seagull—is it friend or foe?" Dave never heard the response as the signal was lost when a fast-moving front disrupted cell tower service across the Aleutian Islands.

"I fear that I have involved these children in some hazardous activity beyond the realm of historical investigation," Dave fretted to his mate.

"Do not worry—the Inua has no fear of adversity. I sense these young ones carry his spirit."

"I hope you are right, Hanta."

CHAPTER 6

The Harbor Mogul

Charlie Vogel was a tycoon and entrepreneur. He was born in New Brunswick, Canada where his father was an accountant and part-time fisherman. A gifted student, he methodically worked his way through high school, college, and eventually business school at the University of Toronto. After graduating at the head of his class he found employment at a top consulting firm for six years before he bought a failing mattress company from a former client. By leveraging the company's assets and painfully reducing employee headcount he promptly increased profitability, rebuilt the company name, and sold it to a British conglomerate for a fortune.

At age fifty-six he moved to Maine to be closer to his roots and began buying up local restaurants, golf courses, and marinas to assert himself as a presence in the communities where he now lived. Boothbay Harbor already had his logo stamped on more than one landmark. Business conquests were a straightforward formula that he executed ruthlessly along the economically depressed seacoast. Yet he found himself unfulfilled and longed for new challenges, so he threw himself into the underbelly of hidden treasures and ancient legends of piracy on the Gulf of Maine. Charlie seemed captivated by a tale he had heard as a boy about a dying sailor from a crew of corsairs, who claimed that a treasure trove had been hidden somewhere on an island near Linekin Bay. Throwing caution to the wind, he spent nearly a million dollars excavating more than one failed site around Damariscove Island, before setting his sights on Bushytail after hearing stories about its caves and unexplored topography. That exploration could not be easily commenced, however, as Bushytail had an association and village corporation that quietly controlled any such undertakings that might occur on the Island. If he could substantiate the existence of pirate activity on the Island, then he would take more assertive action in his quest, but until then he needed the assistance of someone who could furtively direct the exploration and search for clues. A person who could influence the activity of would be treasure hunters without raising the attention of the Island's close-knit community.

· · ·

Robin Grant worked for the Maritime Museum for nine years before being promoted to head archivist, a slight that bothered her more than anyone realized. She majored in anthropology at Bates College and later earned her master's degree in liberal arts with a concentration in Museum Studies from Harvard, so she quietly fumed as other less qualified persons advanced ahead of her professionally. Not so much among her colleagues at Bath, but friends and professionals in positions at the Peabody-Essex Museum in Salem or the Constitution Museum in Charlestown who ascended through the ranks far more rapidly with inferior resumes. Why it was one thing to earn more because you worked for a more prestigious institution, she thought—but quite another to do so without the same comprehensive intellect. In truth, she was pushy and vain which did not endear her to her peers who accepted her brilliance but resented her condescending ways. So, in early spring when a mutual acquaintance asked if she would be interested in doing some "moonlighting" for the ubiquitous Charlie Vogel, her interest was aroused, and she was curious enough to meet the man.

"May I pour you a glass of red wine Miss Grant, a blend from Tuscany?"

"Yes please." Vogel held the wine glass by the bowl and not the stem, a pet peeve to Robin—an annoying habit she attributed to the vulgarians of new money."

"As you may have heard I am not your average businessman. I take risks that most avoid, I follow my instincts down roads others deem to be dead ends, and there's a stubbornness about me that contradicts conventional thinking, all in the chase for exceptional returns."

"Your reputation precedes you Mr. Vogel."

"My reputation is about to change Miss Grant, as I pursue new ventures. You see, I have embarked on a quest for hidden treasure along this rocky seacoast. A search for the holy grail of piracy that has frustrated dozens of treasure hunters from Oak Island to the Isles of Shoals."

"Pardon me for saying this Mr. Vogel, but rumors are swirling that you abandoned a similar treasure hunt at Damariscove."

"As I said I was born stubborn, Miss Grant. The lessons learned from that mission plus the procurement of new clues have altered my course three and a half nautical miles north to Bushytail Isle."

"How interesting. Bushytail has been a summer colony since the late nineteenth century. I can't imagine how such a treasure could have gone undetected after all these years—are you sure about the location?"

"I have a strong intuition about this Island Miss Grant. I sense that this is where the prize awaits. Not a gut feeling mind you, that is quite different. This is what I call Vogel intuition—the subtle knowing, without having any idea why you know it. It's an inner voice I have that's always steering me in the right direction."

"I take your point Mr. Vogel, but how can I possibly be of assistance to you?"

"I asked my contacts to find someone who can, through unorthodox networks and search capabilities, identify and recruit by whatever means necessary, certain agents who can act as our eyes and ears in this reconnaissance. A summer native would be ideal. Beyond that, I will not tell you how to conduct your business, that is for you to determine. What I can tell you is that if successful you will be handsomely rewarded for your efforts, which my assistant will explain together with other details of this assignment. And I would be remiss, Miss Grant, to omit the point that I also have considerable sway among members of your museum's board."

So, there it was, Charlie Vogel was offering her the opportunity of a lifetime. All she had to do was to dig into her vast web of influencers and contacts, canvass the nearby peninsulas, coves, and offshore islands that attracted century old sea raiders for clues, then find the right operatives to conduct a covert exploration of Bushytail. If she came up empty, she could blame the results on Vogel's monomania. If she somehow found evidence of pirate activity or, best of all worlds, an actual discovery of booty, her reputation and professional standing would be burnished beyond her dreams.

After starting her research, she quickly narrowed her focus to the pirate Dixie Bull and by June she had uncovered the existence of the Gavin Ogg diary. Using the museum's ancestry software and a deep Google search she was able to establish a connection to Davidson Ogg in Alaska and was debating how to engage him. There had been some acrimony between the Museum and his father over the ownership of the diary that could make things awkward, so when she received an inquiry from Emma Steele of Bushytail Isle it was like a windfall. The name Steele was not unknown to her, and after a few phone calls, she confirmed that Emma was the granddaughter of Fenton Steele, a retired professor of anthropology at Columbia University, and a summer resident at Bushytail. After weighing their exchange of correspondence, as well as her intellectual lineage, Robin decided it was a good gamble that she was bright enough to not only take the bait but also be receptive to the several clues that she would judiciously drop, and thereby blaze a trail that would reveal any secrets the Island had hidden away. What's more, by cleverly steering her to Red Dog 49, she might uncover whatever information the Ogg family artifacts may hold.

CHAPTER 7

Scots Gaelic

Dennis grasped a work lamp they rescued from a corner in the shed while Emma slowly moved the map back and forth over the incandescent bulb. "If you administer just enough heat it should create a chemical reaction that will release carbon into the air causing oxidation. After a few minutes, the ink should turn soluble, and with any luck, the color will darken." Her eyes glanced up at Dennis, "Let's take our time, we don't want the paper to get so hot that it burns." Gradually, writing appeared on the parchment. Emma placed the map on a table, and they began to examine the characters closely. A line labeled "Plaintext" recited the alphabet in the usual sequence, while below a line marked "Ciphertext" swapped a seemingly random set of 26 letters that created a substitution cipher that was self-reciprocal. Thus, if W substitutes for d, then D substitutes for w. To decipher the encryption, one would use the cipher key to construct the ciphertext alphabet and substitute the plaintext letter for each ciphertext letter."

Dennis's mathematical mind attacked the code as if it were a puzzle, rearranging the symbols before him into a logical plaintext order according to the key. From there the process of decoding the cipher was straightforward. With pencil in hand, he attentively wrote out the solution letter by letter:

CREAG NAN LINNTEAN

He gave Emma a perplexed look. "This can't be right—let me double-check to make sure I followed the substitution key accurately." Dennis painstakingly repeated the progression, then slumped dejectedly in the chair. "It's gibberish, nonsense—the whole affair is a hoax," he muttered irritably.

"Not so fast. Let's be patient and examine this a little more closely." Emma studied the words, then read them aloud to herself phonetically.

"That doesn't sound like any foreign language I've ever heard," Dennis grumbled.

"Certainly not any modern language that we were taught. Didn't Robin Grant say that Gavin Ogg was a Scotsman?" Dennis slowly lifted his languid frame upright then gave Emma that *you did it again* look.

"Of course, and if he was a Scot, he undoubtedly would have possessed some mother tongue besides English—what the Dickens would that be?"

"And when we figure that part out, all we have to do is find a translator," she said sardonically. A screen door slammed, and Grandfather wandered through the mud room and into the kitchen.

"I see you two haven't lost any time looking over that old chart—but why do you have my hand lamp in here?"

"Funny you should ask Grandfather." Emma wasted no time filling him in on her brief phone conversation with Davidson Ogg and their experiment in invisible ink detection.

"We think we solved the cipher but there is one more gap we didn't count on—the message is in some other language utterly foreign to us. We made a blind bargain that it is some ancient Scottish dialect, but we don't know how to prove that deduction or find a translator even if we could."

"May I take a look at what you have?"

"Of course, Grandfather, that's why you're here. You're my first and last recourse whenever I hit a roadblock." Grandfather offered a faint smile then sat down and studied each word. After a minute he wordlessly leaned back in his chair, removed his eyeglasses, and meticulously cleaned each lens before speaking.

"I think your instincts are sound. The letter mix in these words have patterns that look Gaelic to me although not a part of my vocabulary. You need to give this to someone skilled in linguistics."

"It's not likely we are going to find someone of that profession here on the Island—is there somewhere else can we look?"

"Well now that you ask, I have another idea. Why don't you show this to Jock MacLeod, he's a proud Scotsman if ever there was one, and he's made several visits to the Highlands exploring his ancestral roots. He just might be of help."

.   .   .

Dennis wanted to scrub down and rinse out his boat at the float, so Emma detoured their route to a shingle style house with a broad porch that sat squarely on steep ledge overlooking the cove. The cottage owners were just finishing a light lunch and were delighted to find visitors ascending the rocky path and steps.

"Why Emma Steele and Dennis Clark, what nice surprise to see you both, what brings you to MacLeod Nine as we like to call this place?"

"Nice to see you, Mr. and Mrs. MacLeod," they said in near unison. "We stopped by to ask a favor of Mr. MacLeod. We have something that needs translating, a collection of foreign words that we think could be Scottish Gaelic. My grandfather suggested that you might be able to help."

"Well, I can't promise how much help I can be, but let me take a look." Emma handed him the sheet of paper.

"This is old Scots Gaelic all right, but I can't translate it. I know a few words and phrases, but these are unfamiliar to me. Let me copy them down and I'll email it to my relatives in Inverness—they might have to ask around, but they will find someone who can translate it for us. What is this all about?" Emma and Dennis exchanged eye contact.

"Umm it's kind of an ancestry project we're doing for my grandfather's friend, Davidson Ogg—we found these ancient words written down somewhere and are more than just curious to learn their meaning. They could be considered a primary source in our investigation." Emma wasn't being deceitful, but it was best to keep their real purpose unclear for the time being.

"I'll send this off tonight—I should hear back in a day or two."

CHAPTER 8

The Professor Emeritus

Fenton Steele was seventy and on the leeward side of retirement, teaching two four-credit courses as an adjunct professor at the University of Southern Maine. It was an ideal plan for winding down a forty year career as an Ivy League educator—departing a great urban university for the vibrant, charming, coastal community of Portland. He was respected and admired by the USM faculty, so much so that his contract was rewritten to abide by teaching schedules that would not interfere with his summer at Bushytail. Nonetheless, he was professionally accommodating by nature, so when a two-day conference was slated for July by the New England Anthropological Society to be hosted at Bowdoin College, he readily accepted an invitation to participate as a speaker.

The conference opened on a Monday. At daybreak, Dennis ferried him to the Harbor, before he drove his eight year old Nissan Pathfinder to Brunswick as he was on the program for one of the morning sessions. His topic was New Trends in Ethnographic Fieldwork, which basically meant data collection and analysis, and the auditorium was packed, the result of both subject matter and speaker. He lectured for ninety minutes until there was a break with coffee and croissants served in a small, crowded atrium. Conversing with several participants, he noticed out of the corner of his eye, an artful brunette threading her way through a mass of elbows and coffee cups, until she stood before him.

"Your presentation inspired me today Professor Steele—may I call you Fenton? I'm Robin Grant, an admirer, business consultant, facilitator, and overachiever—which is to say, I'm not married because I've never found the perfect man—and your radical approach to observational data collection fascinates me. I want to know more about the renowned gentleman who possesses such a strong and distinctive ethos—and this is a long way of saying I'd love to have dinner with you." Fenton Steele stared at her for several seconds with wide eyes and raised eyebrows that lent an affable expression of surprise. "Well, are you going to say something?" she demanded. She was a handsome woman, fortyish he decided, with dark brown eyes, and a schoolgirl figure.

"I was waiting for you to catch your breath," he answered. She remained wittingly muted. "Well Miss Grant, ahh, I mean Robin you have the advantage. I have no plans for this evening but…"

"Perfect, I'll pick you up at a quarter to six. Don't worry about reservations I've already made them at Maxwell's in Bath."

.   .   .

Robin was relaxed and refined in sundress and sandals as she set out to pick up her date for the evening. She mentally rehearsed her strategy to steer the dinner conversation toward his granddaughter's search for clues at Bushytail Isle. College professors were, as a rule, analytical and literal, but she sensed this one's intuitive nature would deflect any attempt to coax privileged information, so she decided to take a circuitous approach. First, she would put him at ease—let him chill out and discover shared interests, like the theater, summer reading books, or baseball—*they all loved baseball*, she thought to herself. Then she would flatter him, ask him how he managed to stay so trim and attractive, what his secret was to emotional fulfillment. The latter was the kittenish one—a faint nudge to his napping romantic energy.

.   .   .

Robin pulled down the sun visor and flipped open the vanity mirror, checking eye makeup and hair for any imperfections when she arrived at Chamberlain House, a modern student residence that served as housing for conference participants who eschewed Brunswick's hotels for more spartan lodging. She understood punctuality wasn't so notable to a college professor as the impression being late gave, so she was at curbside promptly at five forty-five o'clock.

"Climb in your chariot awaits!" Emma's grandfather stared for a moment at the Porsche 911 idling before him, took a deep breath and lowered his frame to near ground level before twisting and flexing his body into the passenger seat.

"I feel like I'm in a guided missile with wheels," he grunted. Where's the harness in this thing?"

"It's called a seat belt handsome, reach over your right shoulder—and don't worry I'll keep it under ninety." Robin effortlessly worked the clutch and stick, changing gears in rapid succession as they sped along U.S. Route 1. "I bought this car from my broker. He said to me one day: 'I just made you a hundred thousand dollars on that biotech stock—why don't you buy my Porsche?' And I did."

"So, you're an impulse buyer."

"Not really, but whoever dreamed about owning a Nissan?"

"Certainly not I," he bellowed above the scream of the rear 3.8 Liter engine. A comfortable silence followed—before she spoke.

"I'm looking forward to an evening of casual dating, Fenton. I feel somehow safe around you and I want to get to know you better." She smiled and placed her hand on his.

"I'm not sure how to respond—I suppose I will have to trust my instincts." He sensed he was entering another domain—a neglected space that slumbered until now, riding inside a darned saloon car. It was eight years since Maggie passed away. He had never given any thought to exploring matters of the heart, suddenly it seemed like a balm to loneliness.

They arrived at their destination, a two story comparatively old building with a red awning above the doorway that proclaimed this was Maxwell's Restaurant. The maître d' greeted Robin amiably before guiding them swiftly to a table near the back, hardly isolated but far enough away from the kitchen that the pots and pans would not disturb their conversation.

"The oysters here are out of this world—do you like oysters? They're an aphrodisiac you know—harvested fresh from the Damariscotta."

"Of course, I do. They're an acquired taste dating back to prehistoric times, and oysters have been cultivated in Japan since 2000 B.C."

"My Lord, we can't get your mind out of academia and on to more intriguing topics Professor? Tell me, how did you come to be the world's most renowned Ivy League anthropologist?" He ignored the exaggeration.

"I'm afraid there's nothing too romantic in that story. I began my studies at Dartmouth under the tutelage of a professor named Stanley Broder who specialized in Native American cultures. After graduation, I spent two years of active duty in the Navy before returning to earn my doctorate. My dissertation was on the pre-history of New England. It got the attention of one of Stan's research collaborators at Columbia, which led to four decades as a teaching professor and research consultant." He noticed her glassy eyed gaze. "Sorry, I didn't mean to bore you."

"Adore me, don't bore me. I am quite mesmerized by your course of life—every time you reveal something new, I find myself wanting to know more. So, tell me about your inner self—your dreams, your aspirations, the emotional karma that leads you to where you are today."

Where to begin he thought. All those passions started and ended with Maggie. She was smart, witty, and beautiful—not in a glamorous sense—she possessed a natural beauty. She rarely wore makeup, and it suited her. She turned him down the first time he asked her to marry, but he was used to staying with a problem—it just took a little longer. They were charmed by Bushytail Isle after they were invited by Maggie's college roommate to come visit. They returned every summer and bought a house five years later. It was a tired, compact cottage that they reawakened over time—a place where memories were made, and laughter and a love of friends were the only rules. They raised two children together, managed the challenges and rewards of living in New York City, and still found time to explore Muscongus Bay. Years later, he would sit for hours through her chemotherapy sessions, reading aloud from a favorite book—usually a non-fiction best seller but sometimes a trashy romance novel. When the day came to die and she opened her eyes one last time, he held her hand, gently kissed her forehead and whispered, 'until we meet again.'

The evening's Quixotic spell was abruptly broken.

"Honestly, there's really not a lot to tell—endless research projects with brainy graduate students, ballet and piano lessons for the kids, an appreciation for the theater with my wife, and occasionally a Rangers game at Madison Square Garden with a buddy who has season tickets. Pretty much Joe Blow in the Big Apple. But let me turn the table—how did you get into the museum business?" Robin's smile vanished, ousted by a facial expression that divulged surprise.

"How did you know? I never mentioned the museum."

"Your name was familiar to me. I believe you assisted my granddaughter in a history project she was researching." His arched eyebrows expressed curiosity toward the act of omission.

"I serve so many museum patrons every week—yet I should remember—what was her name?"

"Emma Steele, she was looking for information about eighteenth pirates on the Maine coast." Robin pursed her lips and pensively gave a downcast glance.

"Emma Steele, hmm—oh wait I remember her. She came into the museum a few weeks ago with a young man. I should have put two and two together and made the Bushytail Isle connection. I'm a little bit embarrassed. I never brought up my affiliation with the museum because I am trying to establish a separate persona as a business consultant and the two fields seem incompatible to most outside the profession."

"Did I mention I was from Bushytail? I guess I'm getting a little forgetful too."

The rest of the evening passed cordially. Robin tried to pay the check, but her dinner companion wouldn't hear of it—"Old school" he said. The drive back to Brunswick was fleeting and quiet. She pulled up to the Quad to let her passenger off when there was a sudden *splat,* and a white and grey mess oozed across her windshield. Fenton looked up in time to see a large seagull hovering boldly into the wind before banking sharply and disappearing into the night.

"Oh gawd!" Robin cried out, then cursed.

"They say it's good luck," he said with a smile. "I had a lovely evening Robin, I wish you only the best."

CHAPTER 9

The Isle of Skye

"It translates literally to Rock of Ages according to my cousin Fiona, possibly referring to a small hamlet called Uig on the Isle of Skye in the Highlands. It's a remote and rugged place on the western shore where the Scots have raised sheep for centuries."

"Thank you, Mr. MacLeod. I'm not sure how that helps but every clue goes into our collection since it may add up to something later on," Emma said half-heartedly.

"But wait there's more. Fiona is part of a genealogy guild that studies Scottish surnames. She noted, with some measure of intrigue, that your friend Mr. Ogg's name is the anglicized form of a nickname from the Gaelic, Uig–which is, of course, the name of the aforementioned hamlet."

. . .

"So, Gavin Ogg could have hailed from the village of Uig, how does that help us?" Dennis wondered aloud.

"I feel as though I need to paint a picture of this man in my consciousness—outside of my dreams," said Emma. "I think he is the key to this whole mystery and the more I learn about this person who chose to occupy this Island in its colonial infancy the more I can understand his motives and the triumphs or even the failures in settling here, treasure or no treasure."

"Well let's see what Wikipedia tells us about Uig." Dennis quickly targeted his online source and began reading and summarizing at once. "It's one of the four parishes on the Isle of Skye which looks pretty isolated even today. It says that it was a busy place until after the Second World War. Fishing is prevalent but even more so is shepherding—there are still more sheep in Scotland than there are people so that's no surprise," he added as he drilled down a little deeper. "The thing about island sheep is they don't require a lot of attention. If you're raising livestock on the mainland, you have to buy grain, contain the animals, and protect them from predators. The island sheep are kind of self-sufficient, grazing on grass and weeds and living off the land, and it says here that on the northernmost islands of Scotland, the sheep eat nothing but seaweed."

"That's pretty interesting," Emma remarked, "because I've heard that in addition to the Abenaki, Bushytail was inhabited by shepherds since before the Revolution." Dennis swiftly diverted his search engine to Bushytail Isle.

"Yep, the Island was deeded to Newagen, which is what the Europeans called Southport, for the sole purpose of keeping and raising sheep."

"So, Gavin Ogg could have returned to Bushytail because it reminded him of home. A place where he might transplant his roots and raise sheep on this rugged but beautiful coastal Island in the Atlantic. He had no taste for piracy, Robin Grant thought he was conscripted, and Mr. Ogg said that he deserted ship in Machias to gain freedom and independence, not for gold and treasure."

"If that is true, then what is our mission? And where do we go from here?"

"We follow the clues and see where they lead us. There's something at the end of this rainbow Dennis, just maybe not a pot of gold."

.   .   .

Amid a deep sleep, Emma's vision recurs. The first morning light warms the whole Island, and it brings with it a calm kind of peace. Her eyes survey the landfall. Where once were cottages—shrubs and trees have been grazed into oblivion leaving wide expanses of pasture dotted with flocks of sheep. At first, the animals scatter but after a while, it's as though she can walk through them and be almost invisible. Lambs with clean, lustrous, shiny, beautiful, island wool abound. She lifts one and gently embraces it to her breast before releasing it to the safety of the ewes. There is bleating amidst the rhythmic sound of ocean waves that is magic—in a foggy, wind-swept, shadow of a dream.

CHAPTER 10

The Compass Rose

Charlie Vogel was impatient when he learned of Robin Grant's futile efforts to gain any insider information from the Professor or of the progress of the youthful detectives who seemed to be making headway in their Bushytail exploration. Although they were discreet word had leaked back to him through one of their Island confrères, that the talented teens had uncovered clues that could unlock secrets hidden for centuries within the scenic and serene Island. He was also certain they had gained important historical information from the Ogg family progeny in Alaska, and through casual cocktail conversation at the Yacht Club, he had learned of their request for help in translating a cryptic message that was written in some archaic language. The time for bold action was at hand, he decided—a call to the *Boothbay Register* was necessary to stir the pot.

It was a quiet Friday until the chaos erupted. Emma was returning from a morning sail and watched from the cove. People feverishly gamboling up and down the paths and boardwalks in all directions, some with shovels and hoes, others with carts filled with all kinds of gear from survey tripods to soil probes. She raced toward the cove beach where she spied Mrs. MacLeod with a metal detector and headphones slowly canvassing the sand from one end to the other. Above at the ball field, Judy Thompson and her little brother were busy operating a drone with some sort of camera equipment affixed. Suddenly a man she had never seen before rushed by, wearing a sun cap with a long neck cape, and a backpack loaded with hiking gear. Moments later Dennis emerged from the rosa rugosa that skirted the narrow sidewalk, shaking his head in disbelief.

"It's on the front page in today's newspaper. That rich guy, Charlie Vogel, announced to the world that there was a fortune in hidden treasure on Bushytail and that whoever helped him find it would get a share of the prize. Half the Island has gold fever—and that's not all. He let it slip that certain competing agents, recruited by the Maritime Museum, have secretly uncovered proof of the existence of pirate activity that points to Bushytail. It's not going to take long before suspicious eyes are cast in our direction." Before Emma could respond a loud thrum reverberated across the cove as a small flotilla of boats laid siege to the float as well as any unoccupied moorings, delivering a mass of fortune hunters to the Island's shoreline like ants at a picnic. "Where can I get a treasure map?" shouted one lady clad only in a bathing suit and flip-flops as she strode up the walk from the boathouse.

"There are no maps," shouted a passing gentleman with a British inflection, "just clues, clues that are riddles posed by the pirate, himself."

"Where can I find them?"

"Here" he cried, pulling a stack of paper from the deep pocket of his cargo pants, and jamming several copies into the flip-flop lady's eager grasp before taking flight.

"Did you hear that accent? Why he must be a Harvard man" she remarked to no one in particular.

"Excuse me," Emma interrupted, "may I have one of those?"

"Of course you can, here you go sweetie." She was off before Emma could thank her. Emma gave Dennis a head nod and they retreated to the Chapel Garden where she read the missive, then recited it out loud.

Find the rose and draw a line
No deviation covered.
The 7th cardinal tells the tale
Lay one edge against the other.

"How do you suppose Charlie Vogel dug up this?" Emma asked.

"I have no idea—but it is going to take some lateral thinking to solve this riddle. Something disruptive and not so obvious is hidden here."

"That's why I admire you Dennis, your mind is a Rubik's Cube." Dennis brushed aside the comment and furrowed his brow in thought.

"C'mon with me to Historical," he mused "I have something I want to show you."

They arrived in a matter of minutes before Dennis located an old nautical chart of the region, which he carefully unfolded and refolded so that the upper right quadrant appeared in plain view.

"While everyone else is rushing around, madly hunting for flowers and birds…"

"Oh Dennis, you smarty pants—it's a compass rose."

"You bet, and every compass rose, as you know, has four cardinal points: north, east, south, and west. Then there are four intercardinal directions: northeast, southeast, southwest, and northwest. Finally, there are the intermediate or secondary intercardinal directions of which there are eight."

"And number seven is south-southwest," Emma interjected.

"And no magnetic deviation from true north to skew the compass bearing," he said flatly.

Spreading out the chart, Dennis grasped a set of parallel rulers and lined up one edge to the compass rose at an angle of 202° then stepped the opposite edge to Bushytail, and with a pencil plotted a course line south-southwest, through the middle of the Island. Emma, wasting no time, aimed her smartphone, switched on gridlines, and produced a perfectly balanced photo image that she could superimpose over a much larger image of the Island on her computer.

"Okay, now that you've saved it for future examination. Let's put everything back in its place and get out of here."

"Shh! Someone's coming." Emma grabbed Dennis by the arm and hustled him into the kitchenette, to a crouching position so they could hear but not see the intruders. Footsteps echoed across the white pine floor beneath hushed voices. Dennis held up two fingers to indicate the number of people advancing toward them.

"What is this place?"

"It's the Historical Society's headquarters, but the Island uses it for multiple purposes."

"Why did you bring me here?"

"To show you this." The voice paused—Emma could hear the flutter of pages turning in a book.

"It looks like a coat of arms. Why is this of any significance to my investigation?"

"This is the Ogg family crest. Seagulls in Scottish heraldry are not common, but they do exist. On this shield a solitary gull glides on a field of blue over wavy lines that represent water. Legend has it that the souls of drowned sailors and fishermen become seagulls and that they provide easement to friends and obstruction to foes."

"Do you believe that Gavin Ogg drowned?"

"It's possible. I found merchant trade records that indicate a shepherd who provided wool from an Island off Newagen was lost at sea around 1720 and that his body was never found."

"And you have evidence that his soul was reincarnated into a bird?"

"I cannot prove that obviously—but birds are routinely seen as portents of pending calamity and even death. In this case, there is a red eyed gull that has endured among the lobstermen who fish the grounds around Bushytail Isle and its cove for decades, and the same bird recently harassed the Clark boy when he was scaling the cliff at Cutter Point."

"How does all of this relate to Gavin Ogg?'

"Look again at the coat of arms. I have researched and closely examined hundreds of these heraldry symbols—this is the only one I've ever seen that depicts a seagull with a red eye."

"That's very interesting. There was a seagull that vandalized the windshield of my Porsche last week. At the time

I thought it was just an odd reflection, but it looked to me as though it had red eyes." The conversation became muffled and distant, and after a few minutes, the sound of departing footsteps was followed by the opening and closing of the front door. Emma and Dennis slowly rose to their feet making sure their gate crashers were out of sight before exiting the building.

"So, what do you think—have we stumbled into the world of spiritualism?" Dennis asked with a bemused look.

"Curiouser and curiouser. Someone else is investing a lot of time and energy pursuing this case and leaving no stone unturned."

"You recognized the voice of her informant," he said knowingly.

"Of course, that touch of magnolia gave her away. I'm not sure what Erika's motive is but she's done an awful lot of research just to help out a local history buff on a weekend treasure hunt. No, she has to have a skin in the game with someone more important to be so collaborative."

"Do you have a theory who our secret agent might be?"

"No, not yet, but I cannot help but think that I've met her before. I just can't figure out where.

·   ·   ·

The sun was setting over Southport when Emma emerged from the cottage with two Diet Cokes, a bag of tortilla chips, and salsa.

"Cocktails and Hors d'oeuvres on the porch at sunset, a cheap and cheerful way to debrief. Where do we begin Dennis?"

"The seagull hypothesis is intriguing to me. I'm kind of a scientist by nature so I don't believe in ghosts but my encounter in the cave with old Redeye was something right out of a myth—like the ancient mariner."

"Mr. Ogg said that the gull you encountered is a symbol of intuition and if we come upon the bird again to trust it as a spiritual sign but be wary of unseen rivals. His prophecy is accurate as to our shadowy adversaries, so I think I will treat our seagull with some measure of spiritual deference. And by the way, *The Rime of the Ancient Mariner* was a poem by Samuel Taylor Coleridge."

"Do you really believe in this reincarnation stuff, Emma?"

"I've never dwelled too much on the afterlife or reincarnation, but I am a spiritual person I suppose—I don't just leave it all to science." Dennis considered her response, but he couldn't come to embrace the thought of a three hundred year old Scotsman captive inside the body of a seagull. He had read that some sea birds could live for fifty years so that could explain the anecdotal sightings by local lobstermen, and old Redeye was a precocious son-of-a-gun, but beyond that, he wasn't so sure.

"The sailor's legend says the spirit provides easement to friends—that would be you in the cavern, and obstruction to foes—like a load of guano on someone's windshield." Dennis laughed aloud and shook his head.

"She who observed it deserved it. Okay, I concede that there is more to old Redeye than modern science can explain, and I need a return visit to the cave. What's next?"

"The premise that Gavin Ogg became a shepherd is definitely credible and I trust the accuracy of Erika's research, and her conclusions even if I don't trust her motives. The fact that he was native to Uig where shepherding was a way of life, and sailed to America in the early 1700s, matches Bushytail's ecological timeline—and just a small cache of treasure could have easily paid for a flock of sheep from a coastal breeder to establish this as a place to live among his sheep and the birds."

"And yet something lies hidden here, Emma. Your dreams put you on this path that is suddenly crowded with conflicting omens. I think it's time for us to map out our own destiny—to go on the offense and flush out the schemers."

"How do we do that?"

"Look here's our course line that we drew through the Island. At 202 degrees it plots directly through cleft rock at the south shore on the enlargement. Now I'm betting that the cipher translation has been revealed to Charlie Vogel and I think we can create a little mischief by offering a few clues of our own."

"Why Dennis Clark, I never knew you to be so Machiavellian, I like the new you already. When do we start?"

CHAPTER 11

Midnight Sun

After *Sitka's crew* returned to Kodiak Island, Dave Ogg took advantage of Alaska's midnight sun to begin sorting through piles of accumulated stuff that was crammed into the small attic in his house. He rummaged for more than an hour before locating the object of his search—a green metal utility chest about 16" long and 8" wide. USN was stenciled on top where it showed several dents and scratches but was otherwise intact. He carried the box down to the kitchen table before pouring himself a cup of black coffee. Two draw latches on either side secured the box with a key latch in the middle marked USA. He knew that any keys were long lost, but his pocketknife served the purpose and the box sprung open with little difficulty. Inside were several manilla envelopes. One particular sleeve caught his eye, and two fingers deftly removed it from the stack. Pursing his lips he blew away twenty years of previously undisturbed dust. The upper left hand corner displayed the initials "ONI" for

Office of Naval Intelligence, while in the center the letters "TS" were stamped in a large, red, plain text—the military acronym for Top Secret. He removed the contents and examined them intently.

Thirty minutes passed before he sat back in his chair, expelled a deep breath, and began to digest all that he had just read.

History, he believed, was simply the changing of events over time. It included major events, such as wars, and the most minuscule events, such as the winning of a high school football game. It took place every second of every day he thought, a process by which one thing leads to another, which leads to another, and so on. It was a cause and effect kind of thing.

The chain of events unfolding at Bushytail Isle was menacing and required his intervention. He placed the documents he had just read into a fresh new envelope and put pen to paper.

Dear Fenton,

I send this to you with utmost discretion—though after 70 years I should think it is declassified information. You are an astute observer of history and will know how to best apply this material—to set the record straight so to speak and promote some measure of accountability for events that transpired a long time ago. Morality must finally be put to the test.

I sense that Emma and her friend Dennis are wise beyond their years, and I hope they will comprehend the reasons behind this mystery that has endured for decades, and forgive my forebears for the fervencies, favorable or unfavorable, whichever the result.
~D.O.

Later that morning, Dave handed an envelope to the mail clerk, at the post office who verified that it had adequate postage, before continuing briskly down the street to Henry's Diner for breakfast, a daily habit when he was landbound.

"It's nice to start the day with a clear conscience Hanta," he said blithely to his mate who glanced up from the menu.

"I stare at this menu every day—even though I know it by heart. You will never change Dave, you are as predictable as the tides and the moon. So you have protected the children at your own peril."

"It's a small risk to me Hanta. I'm too old to hang for revealing secrets that were made before I was born, don't you think?"

CHAPTER 12

Rock of Ages

"I borrowed this hymn book from the chapel, so I hope we can get it back," Emma lamented. Dennis disregarded the concern as he thumbed through the index.

"Here we go, *Rock of Ages* page 115, let's see if your memory is any good—oh yes Emma, this is perfect. Here's the first stanza of the first verse: *Rock of Ages, cleft for me, let me hide myself in thee.*"

"So now we bookmark the page and send the Hymnal anonymously to Charlie Vogel," Emma replied. "He'll swallow the bait I'm sure. I doubt that he'll show his face but whomever his operatives are, they'll tip their hand with some kind of incursion at cleft rock, and we will know exactly who and what we're up against."

"In the meantime, with everyone else focused on the south shore, I'll follow old Redeye back to his cavern at

Cutter Point, as Mr. Ogg prophesied—I think that's our best chance to unravel this mystery, treasure or no treasure."

· · ·

The package arrived unannounced on the doorstep of Charlie Vogel's office, and he reacted summarily with a call to Canada.

"I've received a tip from an unknown source. It's odd but interesting enough that I want you to check it out. If it's for real and leads to the cache of diamonds I want to be sure we get there first before these kids do. But if they somehow get in the way and blow our cover or threaten to reveal the real object of our mission, we're going to have to do whatever it takes to dissuade them from further activity. As soon as we hang up I'll send you an encrypted message that will give you all the details you need. You won't hear from me again until we rendezvous at the marina."

It took Vogel about five minutes to securely encrypt the contents of his email and dispatch it for delivery. He felt a certain buoyancy as he stared out the window of his office, overlooking the Harbor which he now called home. All he ever really wanted was acceptance—and a reputation untarnished by past events. Now the time had come to rid himself of the sins of the father and stake out his own legacy.

Thus far, everything had fallen into place exactly as he had planned. First, a controversial medical procedure that he championed, proved correct when a seventeen year old girl was admitted to the medical center with severe head trauma. The patient's reduced critical thinking, resulting from a ski accident left little to no access to her true memories and diminished rapid eye movement during dream periods. In a clinical trial funded by the Vogel Foundation, an experimental enzyme inhibitor was administered over a period of weeks, increasing her lucid dream rates through hypnograms that allowed her doctors to incorporate dream content. The result was a fully recovered patient and for Charlie, a guileless Island infiltrator with nameless corsairs and forgotten treasure, implanted in her subconscious mind.

Next, he penetrated Bushytail's close knit community, with spies and influencers. Initially, it was Erika at the historical society whose favor he had earned with a scholarship he funded at his wife's alma mater, the College of Charleston. Erika fancied seances at the Ouija board which she used to extort information from eager spiritualists around the planchette. Not only that but she played the chimes, and through a system that she described as a musical morse code, she could send information to Vogel covertly, any night of the week. All he had to do was relax aboard his yacht somewhere between Southport and Bushytail to receive and decode messages as she rehearsed from the chapel. To oversee the mission he hired the clever Robin

Grant, who between other acts of intrigue, conspired with Erika to feed certain clues and offer encouragement so that his unwitting agent might solve the conundrum of Bushytail Isle on her own and lead him to the prize.

Finally, with a classic scheme of deception, he had convinced the world that he was digging for treasure at Damariscove, then like a con artist at a shell game, moved the charade to Bushytail so that he might collect the object of his search while everyone else was raising havoc in a feverish hunt for silver and gold.

Oh indeed, he could feel it—the time for deliverance had arrived. *Carpe diem* he said to himself, seize the day.

The door buzzer interrupted, he pressed a button on his desk monitor and Robin Grant stepped into the office.

"Have a seat Miss Grant and give me some good news. Have you made any progress in determining whether or not our prodigious teenagers are on to something or are they pursuing tall tales like the rest of the ghost chasers at Bushytail Isle?"

"Don't underestimate them Mr. Vogel—they're not just a couple of smart kids, they evaluate obstacles from a different perspective—I call it upside down problem solving. Instead of thinking about what they need, to get what they want—they think about what prevents them from getting what they want. They've been circumspect about the disinformation we've spread, and they've brainstormed their way through it. If they haven't found the location of the treasure already, I think they've narrowed it down and are preparing to do something audacious that will be seen as a masterstroke if they pull it off."

"Masterstroke, that's an unusual word you use Miss Grant, meaning achievement, action, conquest. Those are elements found through ambition, drive, a burning desire to succeed, or better put, a refusal to concede failure. These children have not yet earned their stripes, fought in the trenches, nor suffered the battle scars to outflank Charlie Vogel. I have fought too many wars and vanquished too many adversaries to let Nancy Drew and Joe Hardy stand in my way. Upside down thinking may work in the classroom Miss Grant, but it can only create a difficult situation here. This morning I received an anonymous envelope that contained this hymnal." Robin opened the songbook to a dogeared page, recognized the hymn, and looked up inquisitively.

"Should *Rock of Ages* turn out to be a Trojan Horse, I'm afraid Bushytail Isle will be made to endure severe penalties which was never my intention." Vogel grabbed a jacket from the coat rack and started heading for the door before pausing. "I have always been fond of the old adage *children should be seen and not heard*, Miss Grant. In this case, *never again seen nor heard from*, would be an unfortunate variant don't you think?" Robin tried to disregard the implied threat but could not find it in her conscience to turn a blind eye to anything that might harm the two young prodigies. She felt uneasy and needed to find a way to defuse the situation.

CHAPTER 13

Rappel and Repel

Emma led a party of treasure seekers, around the south shore explaining the theory that the deciphered Rock of Ages clue referred to a hymn composed by an ancient journeyman, who drew his inspiration from an incident in northern Scotland.

"He was traveling along a steep gorge when he was caught in a tempest when he found shelter deep inside a crevice in the rock formation. He was so moved by his good fortune, that he began writing down the lyrics: *Rock of ages cleft for me; let me hide myself in thee.* We think our accidental pirate embraced this hymn and left its title as an epitaph for two reasons. One because it reminded him of his home in the Highlands; and two because he left something of great value within the cleft rock on this Island where he lived out the remainder of his life as a shepherd."

"Do you have an idea what it might be Emma?" a familiar voice shouted.

"Je ne sais pas—your guess is as good as mine, Judy."

"How do we go about unearthing this hidden treasure?" another gentleman called out.

"With great care and respect for our Island's terrain and vegetation," Emma said with as much weight as she could muster. "I want two of our nimblest members to follow me into the cleft while someone observes us from above taking photos and acting as our recorder, documenting everything we do and interpreting every find. We will treat this just as if it were a field study in an anthropology class, the exact scientific approach my grandfather would advocate." Within the hour Emma had a team of Bushytail excavators, data takers, and photographers, examining the narrow opening and looking for artifacts or any evidence of ancient human activity. The search was on.

.   .   .

Less than a mile away Dennis was preparing to rappel his way down to the entrance to the cave at Cutter Point. Only a few minutes earlier he had seen old Redeye pumping his wings over the waves, going into the cliff hollow—now was the time. Leaning back against the rope he slowly walked his way down the cliff face, allowing the rope to slide smoothly through the belay device before carefully descending to the opening. He was about to swing his frame over to the shelf at the entrance when he felt a lurch—a moment later he was in a free fall, hurtling toward the rocks below. The world around him seemed like a slow-motion movie as waves cascaded silently below and the sky receded from view until a harsh jolt rattled every bone in his body, as gravity was abruptly interrupted, and he swung slowly but precariously in his harness more than halfway down the cliff face. Dennis's body hung limp as a ragdoll while he shook off the effects of the force of the nylon safety rope breaking his fall. Adrenalin rushed through his veins restoring equilibrium and composure as he righted himself. He looked around knowing at once that one of the load-sharing anchors had failed while the other held fast. From the summit, he could hear a faint stirring from amorphous trees, then nothing more until old Redeye emerged from the top of the cliff descending swiftly to the inlet and into a floating position in the ocean 20 feet below. Dennis checked his rope for any hitches, then carefully lowered himself to the base of the cliff, *still in one piece*, he muttered before removing his harness. The bird watched, and Dennis returned the stare as though acknowledging some unspecified act of assistance.

"You saw everything didn't you? Was I careless? Did I fail to check my equipment? Was it an act of God?" The bird held eye contact, swimming slowly before the shoreline. "Or did someone or something promote this mishap? Did you play a part in this grim contest? Emma says you provide easement to friends and obstruction to foes." He raised his eyes aloft to the top of the cliff from where his rope dangled listlessly amid the breathless air. *I'm either very lucky or some crazy spirit is watching over me,* he thought. Dennis lowered his gaze—the bird was gone.

.   .   .

"What's that sound?" Emma asked as she stood in the craggy breach. "It sounds like bees—did someone disturb a nest? Oh gosh, I hope not." The work crew shifted their attention to the area surrounding the excavation, girding for an onslaught of insects while the buzz grew louder. "Look!" Judy hollered, pointing to the sky. Three drones spanning about three feet in size, equipped with four propellers, strafed the glacial rock formation arriving at rapid speed before circling and hovering above.

"Are they spying on us?" Emma yelled, "I think they are equipped with cameras."

"Well they aren't toys—they look like military drones to me," Judy shouted above the din. The aircraft circled several times before one descended solo, to the ridge of the wall where it hovered precariously close to Emma's position like an alien spacecraft observing unworthy earthlings. Emma covered her ears with her hands for what seemed like minutes before it rejoined formation, then retreated with its squadron as suddenly as it had arrived. Emma climbed out from the trench and looked out at the vacant horizon. The intruders had vanished, and she could see only a fog bank in the distance, so after all the excitement died down she decided to call it a day to mend frayed nerves and let the weather clear. Judy volunteered to stay behind to help gather up samples and secure the area.

"How did you identify them so quickly as military drones?" Emma asked as they hefted a bench back to its original station.

"My brother is a drone head, He belongs to a UAV club at his school and subscribes to all the magazines and websites. I read them occasionally and the armed forces aspect intrigues me. It's almost like a Star Wars campaign."

"I know they're used as remote weapons in combat, but I thought they were only licensed for recreation or commercial use around here."

"That's true but like everything else, sooner or later the outlaws figure out how to get their hands on the technology and the trouble starts."

"Judy I apologize if I placed you and the others in harm's way. I knew there was some intrigue going on in this treasure hunt, but I never expected any part of this to be as hazardous as today."

"Don't worry about me—spies, lies, and bad guys. I love it."

Emma smiled in response.

"You know I misjudged you, Judy. I always thought you were a bit of a *you-know-what*. I'm so ashamed."

"Emma Steele—you thought I was a *you-know-what*? I definitely thought you were a *you-know-what*." The two friends broke out in laughter and hugged one another. The moment of attachment was short-lived as the buzz of the interceptors returned, this time higher pitched though less noisy, as a fleet of small but swift drones whizzed in like a swarm of locusts. One immediately glanced off Judy's shoulder causing her to spin and fall backwards, hitting her head against the railing above the boardwalk. Emma grabbed a broken tree limb, swinging futilely at the agile and fast-moving attackers like an impulsive fly swatter. From above several of the drones began releasing some kind of gas-like agent. Emma felt irritation in her eyes and throat and began coughing and wheezing. She put a bandana to her mouth and nose then stood paralyzed with fright as a rogue drone bore down on her. Suddenly old Redeye appeared from out of nowhere like a warplane in a dogfight, knocking the hostile aircraft off course and into a pine tree. Darting through the air as two more collided, then giving chase to another, it drove the robots into digital confusion as it fearlessly pecked at their onboard sensors in midair battle. The turmoil continued while the harriers' numbers depleted in a war of attrition until one solitary aggressor began a final assault on Emma. In predatory fashion her feathered protector spied the attack from above and put itself into a dive, striking its prey full force. A fearsome cry resounded as bird and machine collided, rotor blades ripping into old Redeye, spreading feathers and blood, as an ozone-like smell permeated the air from the wrecked aircraft.

Silence abruptly supplanted chaos as Emma looked across at Judy who was sitting upright but dazed. "Are you okay Judy? Let me see, I think you have a nasty bump there. Oh yes, we need to get this looked at." A cool breeze gently touched her skin and made her shiver, and she noticed the trees were veiled in a light mist. She looked over Judy's shoulder toward the ocean. There he was, standing like a wounded warrior just beyond the tree line on the sea-swept rocks. "You stay here Judy," she instructed before she moved slowly but purposefully toward the bird. She was within ten maybe fifteen feet when she gave a short inaudible gasp and put her hand disquietly to her mouth. His wing was broken and contorted at a hideous angle and a bloody mask covered its once white breast.

"Oh Redeye, you brave, brave friend—I'm so sorry," she cried. The bird's breathing was uneven, even as it stared at her with steady, reassuring eyes that conceded its bold rescue. "Wait here," she pleaded as she raced up the path. *Surely this bird could be nursed back to health with the right care and medical attention*, she thought. She grabbed a blanket, certain that she could adequately wrap the injured seagull and safely transport him to a Harbor veterinarian. She raced back toward the shoreline and then gradually slowed to a halt. "Oh no," she whispered—the bird was nowhere to be seen and a fog bank had enveloped the rocks, obscuring visibility to less than fifty feet. "Redeye" she hollered, "Redeye please be there—I have a blanket, I can help." Her eyes moved frantically from left to right, but the fog was thick, and no matter how hard she tried the sound of the waves overwhelmed her cries.

CHAPTER 14

Town Hall

It would be an exaggeration to say that the Town Hall was packed but there were more than enough Islanders assembled to be considered a small crowd when Emma's grandfather entered the room at 6:00 that evening to explain once and for all the heroic and villainous actions that culminated in the day's bizarre events. Most of Emma's army of volunteers were present as well as many of the other interested treasure hunters including the MacLeods. Also in the audience were several members of Bushytail's governing boards, as well as a State Police Detective and the officer in charge of the Coast Guard Station in Boothbay. Emma and Dennis stood silently in the wings as the anxious group waited to learn the facts behind the tumult that had prompted such curious disruption to the usually placid Island. The room was hushed as her grandfather spoke.

"This morning I received a letter from an old friend from my boarding school days, Davidson Ogg. The pouch that accompanied it contained certain privileged documents from his father's Naval career that he felt I should have, given recent events. Eighty years ago Dave's father was a Navy Intelligence Officer stationed in Biddeford, assigned to monitor German U-boat activity during the war. German submarine activity was taken seriously along the eastern seaboard, especially in the Gulf of Maine. Our entire coastline was patrolled by sub-chasers, and as a result, even here on Bushytail, windows were blackened, civilian lookout posts were manned, and curfews were strictly observed.

Then in August 1944, Dave's father was sent to investigate the sinking of U-1229 south of Newfoundland. The German sub had been on a secret mission and successfully landed a single agent, Oskar Vogel, on an Island on the Maine coast just one week before it was discovered and destroyed. Oskar had lived in New York City for 12 years before the war, working as an accountant, before heading back to Germany to train as a Nazi agent. He arrived carrying a briefcase loaded with cash, diamonds, guns, and fake documentation and orders to gather intelligence and radio it back to Germany. When the Navy rescued the survivors from the sunken U-boat they found information revealing the mission, which crew members under interrogation corroborated, and they forwarded it to ONI. Lieutenant Ogg classified it as top secret and initiated what was to be a yearlong hunt for Oskar Vogel who was later suspected of transmitting information on shipyards, airplane factories, and rocket-testing facilities. Lieutenant Ogg concluded that he hid out for a time in a cave at Cutter Point before making his way at nightfall in an inflatable raft to the mainland to begin his spy work. There were rumors that Vogel was ordered to learn what he could about the Manhattan Project, but no proof of that could be found.

When the war ended a year later the Navy lost interest and Vogel disappeared into the Maritime Provinces according to OSI's intelligence, never to be heard from again. Never again that is, until Charlie Vogel learned at his father's deathbed of the act of treason hidden for more than half a century beneath a quiet, unpretentious life in a small seacoast village in Canada. The cache of diamonds that the elder Vogel carried with him was never found, nor traced by the Navy, and was the one piece of undisclosed evidence that Lieutenant Ogg withheld, which if found, could cause the cold case to resurface and splash headline news across the internet. As a result, Charlie planned and executed an elaborate scheme to recover the diamonds and destroy, once and for all any evidence that might link his name with his father's dishonorable past."

"Where's the scoundrel now?" someone shouted.

"He's in custody. I called the Coast Guard, as soon as I realized there could be some kind of danger surrounding the events that were unfolding and they picked up Vogel and his crew on his boat off Fisherman's Island, which contained an arsenal of armed drones and high-tech tracking devices. At the same time, Robin Grant who, for other reasons, had become suspicious of Vogel's motives and intentions notified the State Police who simultaneously put out an APB to detain him until either the DA or the Navy Department claim jurisdiction."

"So are you saying there is no hidden treasure?" Mrs. MacLeod questioned.

"Well, as an anthropologist I can't answer that conclusively. Legends are popularly regarded to be historical but are rarely verifiable. In this case, there is enough recorded history to support the notion of pirates and privateers in the area but like most legends, no hidden riches have ever been found."

So that was it—the unsatisfying truth was told, and like theatergoers at the end of a film noir, they quietly marched back to their cottages, where they could ruminate and form their own conclusions.

· · ·

Emma and her grandfather had a light supper before quietly retiring to the porch. "They say rocking chairs are for dreams and dreamers," he said after a short silence. "They're a place we can go to think about the events that shape our lives. I hope these old wicker rockers, will see you through many sunsets like this one, Emma. A time to think, a time to reflect, and sometimes a time to grieve."

"Why did he have to die, Grandfather? He wasn't just any old seagull—he was the spirit of a forgotten sailor turned sheep herder who found a way to transcend time, to protect us, and to accept us for who we are—the dreamers, the lovers, and the keepers of the faith on this little summer Island that we call Bushytail."

"I wish I had an easy answer for that Emmy, but I don't. But I do believe that everything happens for a reason. I'm a scientist, not a minister but I still have beliefs. I believe in a god of maybe. Maybe there is something out there that watches over us and gives us a little inspiration, a little bit of hope, a little bit of understanding about our purpose in life, right here on this tiny little land mass in the Atlantic.

This evening I disclosed to everyone present, most of what Dave Ogg entrusted to me. But there is one document that I did not share—one that he wanted me to give exclusively to you. I'm told it's a message in rhyme, a declaration of steadfast devotion." Emma hesitated slightly, before unfolding and then examining the linen paper under the dim light of the porch lantern. The handwriting was neat and cursive and surprisingly readable. It was set apart in distinct verses, as though penned at different times, in different inks, with different writing implements. She began reading slowly and deliberately, immersing herself in the words, savoring each rhythmic sound—ideas that could be communicated in no other words than those of the poet.

> *As I have voyaged o'er this world*
> *I've sought this treasure trove.*
> *My ship careened and sails now furled*
> *On an Island, inside its cove.*
>
> *A place where waves like thunder roar*
> *Nigh rocks by winds sou'west.*
> *I fix my boundaries to this shore*
> *My ewes and lambs possessed.*
>
> *The sirens here have summoned me*
> *It's where I've found contentment.*
> *The prize once hidden by this place*
> *Repaid without resentment.*
>
> *Woolgatherer! woolgatherer! Hail to thee,*
> *The sand, the sea, the fleece.*
> *Sun bleached bones in grassy knolls*
> *Repairs thine inner peace.*
>
> *O' Rock of Ages, cleft for me,*
> *My mortal life is ending*
> *Let me hide myself in thee*
> *Eternal flight transcending.*

Emma rocked, quietly staring out toward the ocean after carefully refolding the document and pressing it close to her chest.

"Tonight this poem is mine. Perhaps tomorrow I'll show it to you, Grandfather, and maybe thereafter I'll share it with the world. But for tonight at least, it is mine alone." She rose from her seat and softly kissed his cheek. "Goodnight Grandfather, I love you."

CHAPTER 15

A Gentle Goodbye

The season flew by and before anyone knew it, it was time for Island kids over the age of sixteen to pack up and head for home or to college or whatever autumn obligations might summon them. Dennis and Judy chatted with Emma and her grandfather on the porch enjoying one final sunset before Sunday's boat ride would conclude their summer.

"I hear you have a big date in the Harbor, Professor Steele."

"Relax Dennis, it's not a date in that sense, just a leisurely dinner with Robin Grant. I never did thank her for what she did in helping to hold Charlie Vogel accountable, and it seemed like a good opportunity to tie up a few loose ends." Emma smiled and gave Dennis a wink.

"Well I hope you thank her for us," Judy said. "I don't know where I'd be today if this treasure hunt had gone unresolved. I feel like I gained so many lessons from everything that came to pass—not to mention lifelong friendships."

"How about you Emma? We haven't talked too much about all of this since last July." She paused and looked wistfully at her grandfather.

"I feel as though I've matured so much this summer and in so many ways, Grandfather. My dreams really did lead me to a new appreciation for my time and place on this Island. It's about realizing that everything has value, and everything has beauty. Gavin Ogg was a humble shepherd, a *woolgatherer* is what he called himself. He loved this place for the intimacy and contentment that it brought to his life—a prize he valued more than any treasure on earth. Woolgatherer, that's a word grandmother used when we were little kids running around Bushytail—daydreamers, stargazers, indifferent to the busy world beyond. Woolgathers that's what she called us—and that's who we are, Woolgatherers."

.   .   .

Emma moved from the cabin to the stern, away from the other passengers halfway through the trip to the Harbor. She wanted a few moments to herself to think about the sadness and regret she felt in leaving Bushytail. It happened every August, and she knew she'd be back next year, but there was a certain hollowness this time as if she was leaving behind a part of her that could never be reclaimed. She brooded, standing at the rail, until a sharp unnecessary squawk cleared her head. She shaded her eyes and gazed astern above the wake. A lonesome seagull drifted aimlessly beyond the transom as though tied to a tether, before rising high onto a bed of air and softly dipping its wings from side to side—a wing wave—a gentle goodbye. Emma smiled.

THE END

ABOUT THE AUTHOR

Arthur H. Veasey III was born and raised in Haverhill, Massachusetts. He was educated at Haverhill Public Schools and Governor Dummer Academy, in Byfield, before completing his higher education at the University of Denver in Colorado. *The Woolgatherers* is his fourth novella. He and his wife Susan reside in West Newbury, Massachusetts, and spend their summers on a small Island in the Gulf of Maine, together with their golden retriever Schooner.